Wheaten Puppy Love

Wheaten Puppy Love

Dr. Diane P. Fleming

Wheaten Puppy Love

Copyright © 2024 by Dr. Diane P. Fleming. All rights reserved.

No part of this publication may be reproduced, stored in a retrieval system or transmitted in any way by any means, electronic, mechanical, photocopy, recording or otherwise without the prior permission of the author except as provided by USA copyright law.

The opinions expressed by the author are not necessarily those of URLink Print and Media.

1603 Capitol Ave., Suite 310 Cheyenne, Wyoming USA 82001
1-888-980-6523 | admin@urlinkpublishing.com

URLink Print and Media is committed to excellence in the publishing industry.

Book design copyright © 2024 by URLink Print and Media. All rights reserved.

Published in the United States of America

Library of Congress Control Number: Pending
ISBN 978-1-68486-830-8 (Paperback)
ISBN 978-1-68486-831-5 (Digital)

08.07.24

Dedication

Wheaten Puppy Love is dedicated to my grandmother, mother, and the love of my life. Your help and support were invaluable.

Acknowledgments

I want to express my gratitude to my friends who have provided support, read, and made suggestions, making this book an excellent opportunity for young children. Specifically, Dr. Deborah Daiek, Judith Dubin, Carol Hovsepian, Essie Martin, Vivian Jenkins, and Jackie Urbanovic deserve my gratitude. I would also like to give a special shout-out to two outstanding breeders who generously shared some of their pictures for *Wheaten Puppy Love.* Breeders are special people who utilize unique skills to ensure that Wheatens are healthy and well-bred.

☐ Denise Daniels, the owner of Star Wheatens, resides in Westland, MI. She can be reached at: ddddstar@aol.com

☐ Karli Muller-Brough, owner of Kaler Wheatens, resides in Howell, MI, and can be reached at: dogcoachkarli@gmail.com

Permission was granted via email from the breeders mentioned above to use pictures in the book.

Diane Fleming, author of *Wheaten Puppy Love,* supplied additional photos for this book.

Additional thanks to my editor, Lor Bingham, Calico Editing Services; photographer Shelby Dubin, owner of Shelby Dubin Photography; and Christi Lopez, Graphic Designer, for designing my logo.

Soft-coated Wheaten puppies are born.

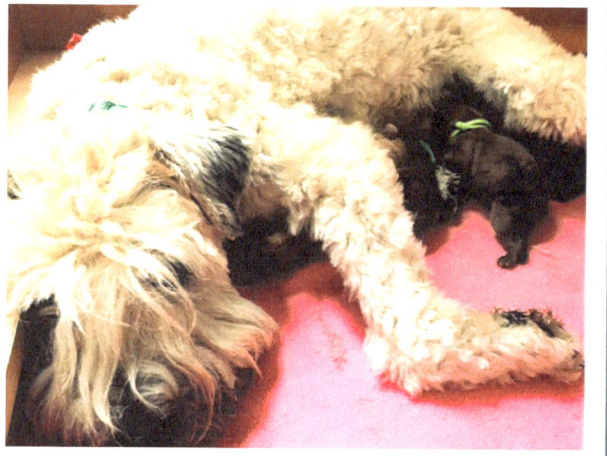

Wheaten puppies have two types of hair:

Irish curly, or straight and soft.

Which hair looks curly to you?

Puppies are born with their eyes closed.

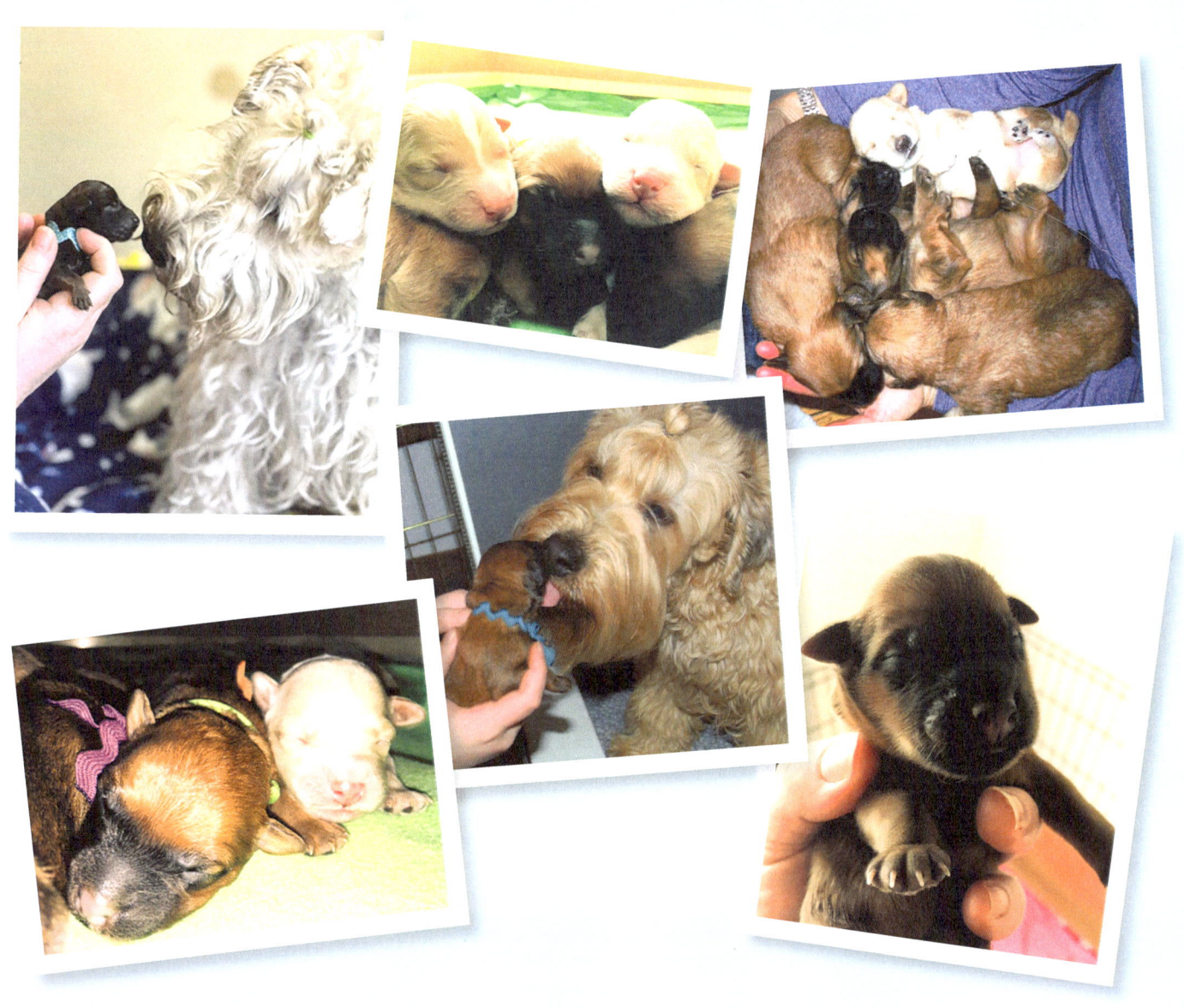

Puppies have big brown eyes and a dark black nose.

Can you point to the puppy's nose?

Puppies are born in different colors. They can be black, brown, or tan.

How many puppies do you see?

As puppies begin to grow, they change from a darker color to a tan color.

Newborn puppies stay with their mom for eight to ten weeks.

Can you count to eight?

Breeders put different color collars on puppies to tell them apart.

Which collar is your favorite?

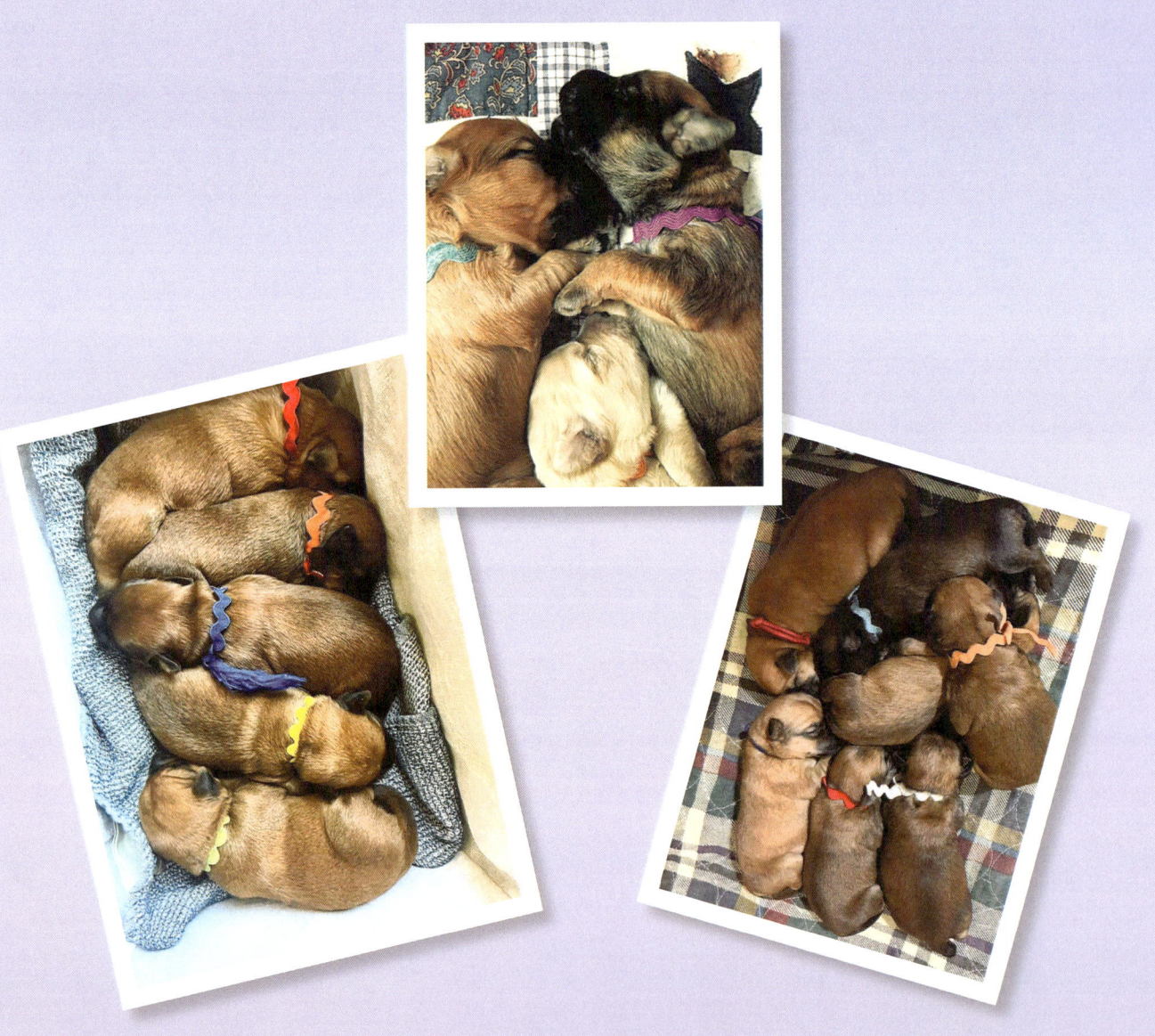

Wheaten puppies are very friendly and lovable.

All puppies like to drink milk ... especially Wheaten puppies.

Do you like to drink milk?

Wheaten puppies need to be bathed, cut, and combed.

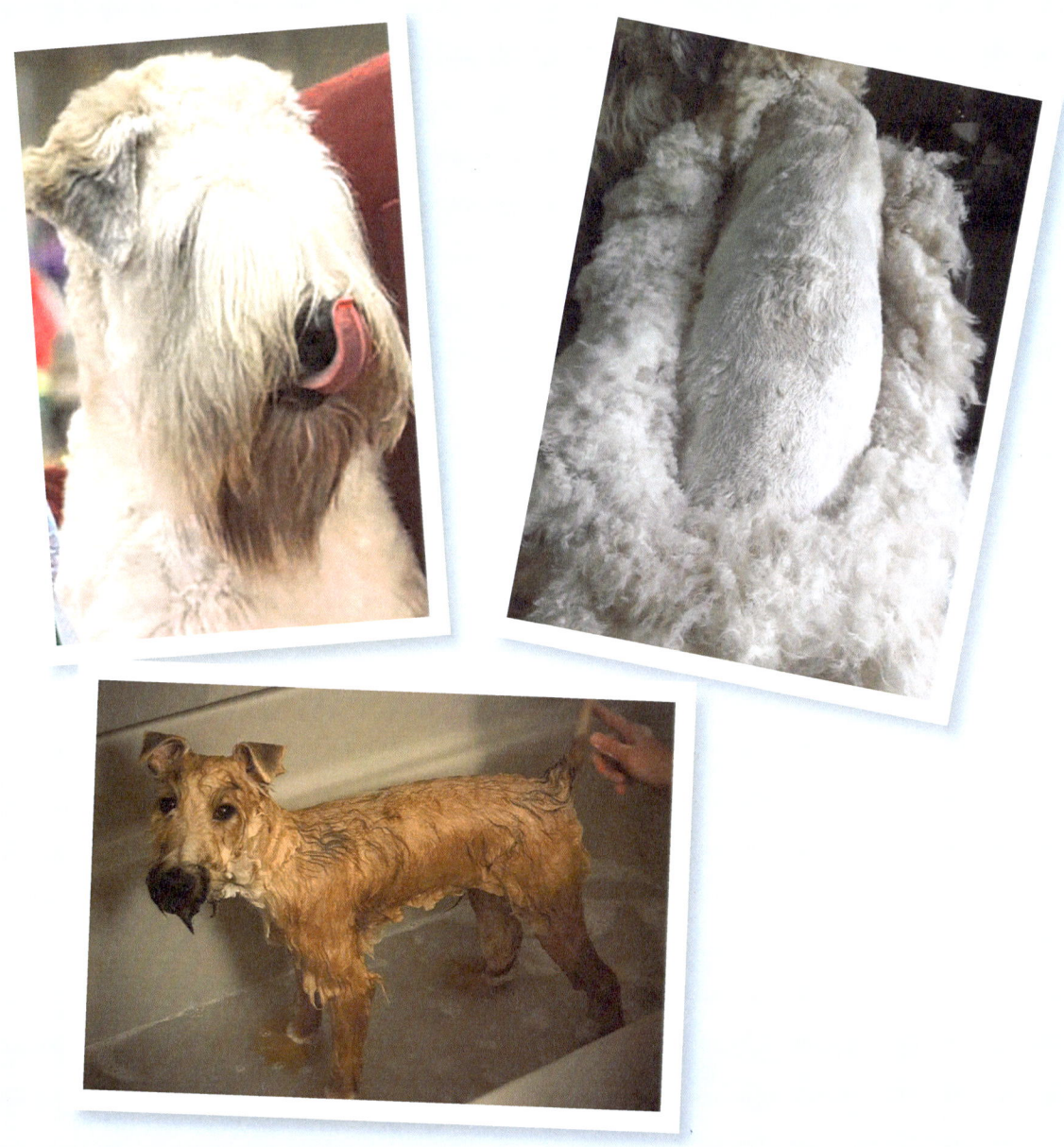

Here are Wheaten's with new haircuts.

At ten weeks, puppies go to their new forever home.

Puppies go to a doctor who is called a veterinarian. Medicine called a vaccination is necessary for puppies to stay strong and healthy.

Look at this puppy traveling in a backpack.

What do you put in your backpack?

This puppy carries his bowl to the kitchen. Some play with their dishes.

Having a crate gives puppies a place of their own.

The puppies play together after they get strong.

Puppies are very active and like to play.

Puppies like to play with toys; some have a lot.

Do you have favorite toys?

Some puppies often wear costumes.

Which is your favorite?

Many owners have their dog's pictures taken with Santa.

All puppies need training. Training can include sit, come, and stay.

Some pure-bred dogs go to dog shows. They get awards.

Puppies love to play in the snow.

Do you like snow?

Puppies can get dirty even playing in the grass.

This Wheaten puppy has a pool.

Have you been in a pool?

Puppies sleep in different positions.

Puppies are involved in many activities.

Puppy and parents. Which one is the puppy?